CHRISTMAS AHOY!

Written by **ERIN DEALEY** and Illustrated by **KAYLA STARK**

PUBLISHED BY SLEEPING BEAR PRESS™

The big harbor bustles with people and light.
The Holiday Boat Parade starts tonight!
From starboard to port, the lighted boats shine.
The judges are ready. The boats get in line.

ONE lighthouse
decorates a sailboat mast.

TWO gondoliers sing of Christmases past.

THREE tugboats chug along like railroad cars.

FOUR surfboard trees shine with holiday stars.

fiVE fishers harmonize, ever so merry.

SIX dancers twirl on the Sugar Plum Ferry!

SEVEN sweet gingerbread houseboats spread joy!

OH BOY!

EIGHT paddling pirates shout,

"CHRISTMAS–AHOY!"

WAIT!

Where's Santa's barge with EIGHT flying reindeer?

Santa is missing?! He's supposed to be here!

Rumors abound! The crowd starts to chatter.

The judges look worried. What could be the matter?

"ARRRR . . ."

say the pirates, at the crest of a wake.

"The reindeer are tired. They needed a break."

WHAT?

No reindeer?

No Santa?

How could this be?

"AVAST,"
say the pirates.
"They're coming. You'll see."

Then in the distance—the clang of a bell!
A yacht glides into the harbor, and well . . .

NINE reindeer chill fore and aft.

What a sight!

LOOK!

TEN flying fish will pull Santa tonight!

Away the fish fly, as the spectators cheer.

"MERRY CHRISTMAS TO ALL—
AND A HAPPY NEW YEAR!"

WHETHER YOURS HAS AN ENGINE,
A SAIL, OR SOME OARS,

SAILBOAT Sailboats, powered by the wind, have been around for over 5,000 years! Egyptians were the first to use sailboats on the Nile, and later the Mediterranean Sea.

GONDOLA Gondolas were first used in Venice, Italy. One oarsman, or gondolier, uses a single oar to move and steer the long rowboat. The very first Boat Parade in Newport Beach, California, began over 100 years ago, with one gondola and eight canoes, inspired by the gondola parades in Italy.

TUGBOAT Tugboats were invented in the early 1800s, after steam-power was successfully used to power watercraft. Tugboats replaced mules as the "muscle" that helped propel canal boats, and eventually barges, disabled boats, and other vessels.

PONTOON BOAT The pontoon boat was the brainchild of Michigan inventor Ambrose Weeres. In 1951, he combined a wooden platform atop two columns of steel barrels welded together end to end, to create a pleasure craft which was way more stable than the conventional fishing boat.

SURFBOARD The concept of the surfboard is not as new as you might think. Over 2,000 years ago, Peruvian fishermen made boats called Caballito de Totora from tightly woven reeds. It is said the fishermen paddled their crafts out into the Pacific surf and used the waves to help push them back to land. According to the Bishop Museum in Honolulu, Hawaii, the sighting of the world's oldest surfboard, as we know it, dates back to 1778-79.

FISHING TRAWLER On a fishing trawler, a net or trawl is used to catch fish as it's dragged through the water. The trawl is set and removed from the water by either a winch or a crew of fishers. The first steam-powered fishing trawler was pioneered in the late 1800s.

FERRY Before bridges were constructed to allow people to cross large bodies of water, ferries were used. The earliest mention is in Ancient Greek mythology. A common image of an early U.S. ferry is one with a steam-powered paddle wheel. Commuter ferries are still popular today.

HOUSEBOAT

A simple houseboat has one or two rooms built on a flat-bottomed scow, usually with a porch or platform on each end. Houseboats can be found in many variations around the world.

SUP/PADDLE BOARDS

Both the gondoliers of Italy as well as fishermen (and later lifeguards) of Israel lay claim to the beginnings of stand-up paddleboards or SUPs. SUPs are also said to have originated with those Peruvian fishermen, over 2,000 years ago. It is said that the most proficient would occasionally stand up on their Caballito de Totora.

RESCUE BOAT

A boat rescue craft is a vessel used to help another boat in distress and/or its passengers and crew. We are thankful for the lifeguards, harbor patrol, and Coast Guard who operate them.

YACHT

The yacht is the invention of the fourteenth-century Dutch, called jaghts. The first Yacht Club in the world, Cork Water Club (Ireland), was established in 1720. Experts say that a yacht should not be defined by its size or weight or style but rather by the fact that it's the only craft specifically designed for pleasure, instead of work.

BARGE

The beginnings of the modern barge date back to the seventeenth century. Most early barges, used to glide along calm rivers and canals, were only meant for one trip. When they arrived at their destination, the barge was taken apart and the lumber used for construction or firewood.

DORY

A dory is typically a flat-bottomed boat with no keel. Fishers from Portugal to Holland used them. Artist Vincent van Gogh sketched Dutch dories that look like small sailboats. Other dories are more like rowboats. Dories were cheap and quick to build and very stackable. This allowed stacks of them to be loaded on a larger ship, launched when they arrived at key fishing grounds, and brought back on board at the end of the day.

ROWING SHELL

In the water sport known as crew, competitive rowing teams row a craft called a shell, usually propelled by eight oars. Crew members row with an oar in each hand. Rowing in six- and eight-oar shells began as a club and school activity in England in the early nineteenth century, and sometime later in the U.S. Organized racing at universities like Oxford and Cambridge began in the 1820s and at Harvard and Yale around 1851. Crew became an Olympic sport in 1900. Today the sport is popular around the world.

This one's for Owen, and all the Kelly/Goddard sailors past, present, and future.
With endless gratitude to Deborah Warren and Sarah Rockett

—*Erin*

For Mackie, a boat friend.

—*Kayla*

Text Copyright © 2023 Erin Dealey
Illustration Copyright © 2023 Kayla Stark
Design Copyright © 2023 Sleeping Bear Press

SLEEPING BEAR PRESS™
2395 South Huron Parkway, Suite 200
Ann Arbor, MI 48104
www.sleepingbearpress.com

Printed and bound in the United States.

10 9 8 7 6 5 4 3 2 1

Library of Congress Cataloging-in-Publication Data on file.

ISBN 9781534111783

Photo credits pages 30-31: © De Visu/Shutterstock, © James Steidl/Shutterstock, © Andrey Mihaylov/Shutterstock, © Anne Kitzman/Shutterstock, © trubavin/Shutterstock, © Split Second Stock/Shutterstock, © Netfalls Remy Musser/Shutterstock, © Aleksei Kochev/Shutterstock, © Koltsov/Shutterstock, © Oleksiy Mark/Shutterstock, © Aerial-motion/Shutterstock, © AlinaMD/Shutterstock, © Andy Roo/Shutterstock, © Ivan Smuk/Shutterstock